Hilde Cracks the Case

HAVE YOU READ ALL THE MYSTERIES?

More books coming soon!

Hilde Cracks the Case

HERO DOG!

BY HILDE LYSIAK
WITH MATTHEW LYSIAK

ILLUSTRATED BY
JOANNE LEW-VRIETHOFF

BRANCHES™

SCHOLASTIC INC.

To my dad, who taught me about being a reporter. To my mom, who never "clipped my wings." To my sisters, Izzy, Georgie, and Juliet, who keep me on my toes. To my Mimi, who loves me with all her heart. To my PopPop, who is a war hero. And to my grandparents, Gina and Arthur Lysiak, who I miss so much and think about every day.

Copyright © 2017 by Hilde Lysiak and Matthew Lysiak
Illustrations copyright © 2017 by Joanne Lew-Vriethoff

Photos ©: cover: spirals and throughout: Kavee Pathomboon/Dreamstime; back cover: paper clip: Picsfive/Dreamstime; back cover: paper: Frbird/Dreamstime; back cover: tape: _human/Thinkstock; 90 paper clips and throughout: Fosin2/Thinkstock; 90 pins: Picsfive/Dreamstime; 90 bottom: Courtesy of Joanne Lew-Vriethoff; 90 & 104: background: Leo Lintang/Dreamstime.

Library of Congress Cataloging-in-Publication Data
Names: Lysiak, Hilde, 2006- author. | Lysiak, Matthew, author. | Lew-Vriethoff, Joanne, illustrator.
Title: Hero dog! / by Hilde Lysiak, with Matthew Lysiak ; illustrated by Joanne Lew-Vriethoff.
Description: New York, NY : Branches/Scholastic Inc., 2017. | Series: Hilde cracks the case ; [1] |
Summary: Nine-year-old Hilde Lysiak is an aspiring reporter with her own newspaper, the Orange Street News, and she is investigating break-ins and missing baked goods—and with the help of Zeus, a little dog with a big bark, she intends to track down the thief who is trying to steal a win in the Bake-Off Bonanza, one of Selinsgrove's biggest events.
Identifiers: LCCN 2016054928| ISBN 9781338141559 (pbk. : alk. paper) | ISBN 9781338141566 (hardcover : alk. paper)
Subjects: LCSH: Reporters and reporting—Juvenile fiction. | Theft—Juvenile fiction. | Dogs—Juvenile fiction. | Detective and mystery stories. | CYAC: Mystery and detective stories. | Reporters and reporting—Fiction. | Stealing—Fiction. | Dogs—Fiction. | GSAFD: Mystery fiction. | LCGFT: Detective and mystery fiction.
Classification: LCC PZ7.1.L97 He 2017 | DDC 813.6 [Fic] —dc23 LC record available at https://lccn.loc.gov/2016054928

10 9 8 7 6 5 4 3 2 1   17 18 19 20 21

Printed in China 38
First edition, September 2017
Edited by Katie Carella
Book design by Baily Crawford

Table of Contents

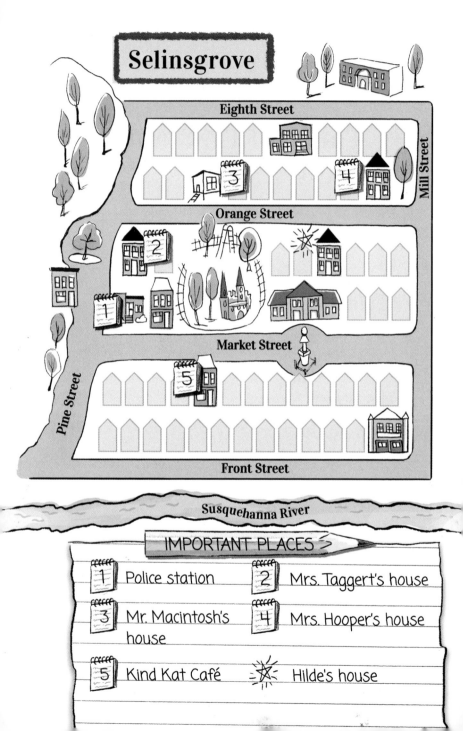

Introduction

Hi! My name is Hilde. (It rhymes with *build-y!*) I may be only nine years old, but I'm a serious reporter.

I learned all about newspapers from my dad. He used to be a reporter in New York City! I loved going with him to the scene of the crime. Each story was a puzzle. To put the pieces together, we had to answer six questions: Who? What? When? Where? Why? How? Then we'd solve the mystery!

I knew right away I wanted to be a reporter. But I also knew that no big newspaper was going to hire a kid. Did I let that stop me? Not a chance! That's why I created a paper for my hometown: the *Orange Street News.*

Now all I needed were stories that would make people want to read my paper. I wasn't going to find those sitting at home! Being a reporter means going out and hunting down the news. And there's no telling where a story will take me . . .

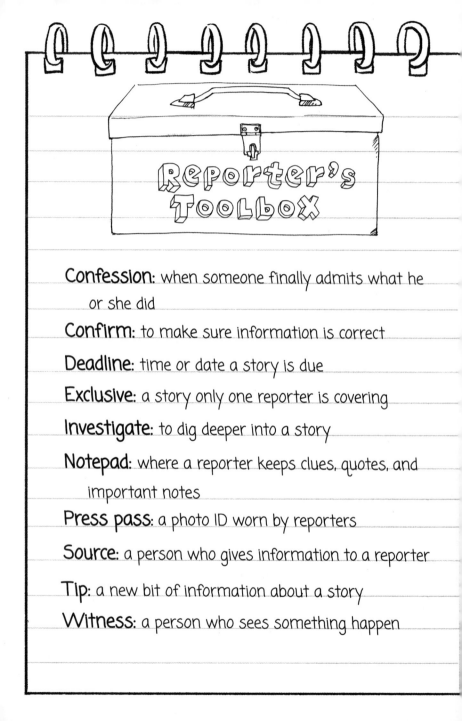

Reporter's Toolbox

Confession: when someone finally admits what he or she did

Confirm: to make sure information is correct

Deadline: time or date a story is due

Exclusive: a story only one reporter is covering

Investigate: to dig deeper into a story

Notepad: where a reporter keeps clues, quotes, and important notes

Press pass: a photo ID worn by reporters

Source: a person who gives information to a reporter

Tip: a new bit of information about a story

Witness: a person who sees something happen

1 Break-in on Orange

There I was, standing outside the Selinsgrove police station in the pouring rain. I needed to get inside, but the door was locked shut. I needed information — fast!

I rang the buzzer.

And waited.

I rang it again.

But the police were still not answering.

I had gotten a tip that someone broke into a home on Orange Street!

Orange Street didn't happen to be just any street. It was the street my family called home.

I needed to investigate right away.

I had hardly noticed the heavy rain during the four-block ride from my house to the police station. I had other things on my mind.

Who? What? When? Where? Why? How?

I knew *when* the break-in happened: *early morning.* But I needed a lot more answers if I wanted to have a story fit for the *Orange Street News.*

The question right now was *where: Where did the break-in happen?* As soon as I found out which house was broken into, I would call my older sister/photographer, Izzy, to take pictures.

The clock was ticking and I was on deadline. My story had to be posted online by 6 p.m. today!

I checked my phone. It was 12:30 p.m.

My hands felt cold. My socks felt squishy.

I rang the buzzer again.

Tick. Tock. Tick. Tock.

A tall police officer answered.

Finally!

2 Mean-agers!

The police officer peeked his head out the door, careful not to get wet. My heart sank. I remembered this guy: Officer Wentworth. He was never helpful.

"Hi, I'm Hilde from the *Orange Street News*," I said, pulling out my notepad. "Could you please give me the address of this morning's break-in on Orange Street?"

The officer sighed. "It is an open investigation."

That's police talk for "I am not telling you anything."

"But the people of Selinsgrove have a right to know!" I said.

"We aren't giving the address out to the press," he said, before closing the door.

I'd just have to uncover the address myself. Time to start knocking on doors! If a reporter knocks on enough doors, answers are bound to follow.

I slung my tote bag over my handlebars and sloshed through a puddle.

I was about to make a right onto Orange Street when I slammed on my brakes.

It was the Mean-agers!

Donnie, Leon, and Maddy: teenagers with rotten attitudes.

I pulled up a safe distance away. That way I could skip all the teasing. Especially their favorite: "Hey, Hilde, how is your cute little baby paper?"

I hated when people made fun of the *Orange Street News*. It isn't *cute*. It's a serious newspaper. And serious reporters always need to make sure they aren't missing out on a story.

So I began eavesdropping . . .

The Mean-agers were talking about a band coming to town.

"I've heard Noise Pollution concerts are epic," said Donnie.

"All three of us are totally going!" said Maddy.

I've seen a few Noise Pollution music videos. The band is just a bunch of angry grown-ups screaming into a microphone.

"Tickets are two hundred and fifty dollars," I overheard Leon say. Then he spotted me and shot a stink eye my way!

I pedaled right out of there. This didn't sound like a story anyway.

I pulled up to the first house on Orange Street, climbed the stairs, and knocked.

An old lady spoke through a crack in the door. "Hello."

Her blue robe and curly gray hair reminded me of my grammy.

I cleared the strands of wet hair out of my eyes.

"Hi, I'm Hilde from the *Orange Street News*," I began.

She smiled. "Hello, Hilde. I'm Mrs. Taggert. What can I do for you?"

"I was wondering if you know anything about the break-in that happened on your street," I said.

"I heard about that," she said, rubbing her chin. "But I don't know anything."

"Are you sure?" I asked. "Any information might help!"

Just as I was about to put my notepad away, Mrs. Taggert began talking.

"Well, I did hear some noises."

My ears perked up.

3 SQUAWK! SQUAWK!

Mrs. Taggert opened the door wider. She looked at me. "You're soaking wet! Are you trying to catch a —"

She meant well, but I had important work to do. It was 1 p.m. and I still hadn't discovered the address of the crime! I had to interrupt her.

"I'll make sure to dry off soon. Now, could you please tell me about the noises you heard?" I asked.

Mrs. Taggert pointed across the street.

"I heard those awful chickens. They were making a ruckus."

"Chickens?" I repeated.

This tip didn't sound helpful. It sounded too weird to be true. But sometimes the truth is super weird, so I needed to investigate every clue.

"Chickens," the old lady repeated. "Roy Macintosh has a bunch of those dirty creatures penned up behind his house. Their squawking woke me up when it was still dark out."

I jotted a note in my pad.

WHEN: Early morning, still dark out

WHERE: Mr. Macintosh's house

NOTE: Maybe the chickens were squawking because the thief was nearby?

"Anything else you remember?" I asked.

"No," she said. "Oh! I have a cherry crumb pie I need to take out of the oven!"

Mmmmm.

I caught a whiff of the pie. I could almost taste the warm sugar crumb topping.

"Wait a minute!" I said. "Are you the Mrs. Taggert whose pie won last year's Bake-Off Bonanza?"

I remembered writing a story about the contest.

The Bake-Off Bonanza was one of Selinsgrove's biggest events! The contest included pies, cookies, cupcakes, and other sweets. This year's contest was later today.

Mrs. Taggert smiled. "Yes, that's me. I'm hoping my pie will win again this year," she said. "Would you actually like to come in for a snack? I have oatmeal raisin cookies cooling off."

I loved all cookies — but oatmeal raisin cookies were my absolute favorite, next to chocolate chip.

And snickerdoodles.

And peanut butter blossoms.

But I had a mystery to solve.

"Thank you, but I have to go," I said.

"Take care, dear," Mrs. Taggert said, closing the door. "This thief could be dangerous."

The rain had stopped and sunlight pushed through the clouds.

Time to investigate the chicken coop!

I grabbed my bike and walked it across the street.

I could see the coop in the backyard.

I opened the latch on the gate. Then —

GRRRRRRRRRRRRRRUFFF!

I heard the biggest, most terrifying bark.

4 Mighty Zeus!

A tiny, scruffy-haired black dog ran up to me.

The dog wasn't terrifying at all — he was adorable!

I was laughing when a large man wearing blue overalls walked over.

"Don't mind Zeus. He is all bark," the man said, smiling.

It was Mr. Macintosh. I had seen him around, but I had never spoken to him before. I didn't know he had a dog.

"I've never heard a dog bark so loud. I thought I was about to become a chew toy!" I said, rubbing behind Zeus's ears.

"People often mistake my little Zeus's bark for that of a dog ten times his size," Mr. Macintosh said. "Now, what can I help you with?"

"I'm Hilde of the *Orange Street News*," I began, taking out my notepad. "I was wondering if I could ask you a few questions about the break-in on your street."

"The break-in," he said. "What makes you think I would know anything about that?"

"Well, I was across the street talking to —" I began to explain.

"Was that old woman complaining about my chickens *again*?" he said.

He suddenly sounded grumpy.

"No — well, kind of," I stammered. "Mrs. Taggert said she heard your chickens making a lot of noise. I thought it might have something to do with the break-in."

"Mrs. Taggert only has herself and all her baking to blame for the noise," he said.

"What do you mean?" I asked.

"She's always baking with her windows open. The sweet smells make my animals go crazy! Especially poor Zeus," Mr. Macintosh explained.

I wrote everything down.

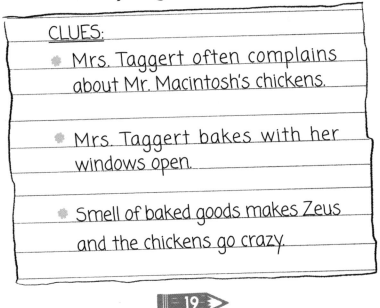

CLUES:
* Mrs. Taggert often complains about Mr. Macintosh's chickens.

* Mrs. Taggert bakes with her windows open.

* Smell of baked goods makes Zeus and the chickens go crazy.

"Would it be okay if I check out your chicken coop?" I asked.

"You're certainly nosy," he said. "And you ask a lot of questions."

"It's a reporter's job to ask questions," I answered.

I knew if I took myself seriously, other people would take me seriously, too. I looked him straight in the eyes.

"Be my guest — take a look in the coop. You'll see my chickens are just as well-behaved as my dog," he said. "I have nothing to hide."

Zeus followed me to the coop, and we stepped inside.

It was a mess! Feathers covered the dirt floor.

"Um . . . Mr. Macintosh?" I called out. "Is your coop always this messy?"

He rushed inside.

"Oh, no!" he gasped. "My eggs! They're gone!"

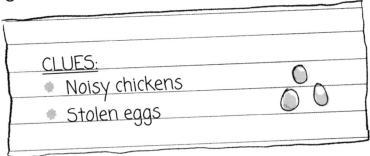

CLUES:
* Noisy chickens
* Stolen eggs

5 Stolen Eggs

"**H**mmm," I said, looking around Mr. Macintosh's chicken coop. "It looks like your eggs have been stolen. But at least the chickens will lay more tomorrow."

"That's not soon enough!" he said. "I needed those fresh eggs to bake my award-winning cheesecake for today's Bake-Off Bonanza."

"I remember that cheesecake!" I said. "Didn't it win second place last year?"

"Yup," said Mr. Macintosh proudly. "And the year before that, it beat Mrs. Taggert's cherry crumb pie. The old lady still hasn't gotten over it!"

Bake-Off Bonanza
ORANGE STREET NEWS
WINNER

His face clouded over. "*Now* what will I bake for the contest?" he said.

"I don't know," I replied. "But I *will* find out who did this! Did you see or hear anything strange?"

"I guess I did see something strange," he said. "I noticed a broken plate and some smashed cupcakes in the road over there."

I looked where he was pointing. I saw several cupcakes scattered near a broken plate. And there were crumbs all over the street.

"Thanks for the tip!" I said.

WHAT:
* Broken plate
* Smashed cupcakes

WHO:
* A baked-goods-loving thief?

"You better check it out soon," Mr. Macintosh replied. "I'm about to take Zeus for a walk and he has a sweet tooth."

"I'll investigate right away," I said. "Also, can my sister Izzy come take pictures of your coop?"

"Sure, whatever helps catch this thief," he said.

I shot Izzy a text.

OOOO 📶   2:00   🔋

Hey, Izzy! Get to the corner of Orange and Pine fast! Take pics inside the chicken coop! Then meet me near the broken plate in the road!

Okay, hotshot.

Tick. Tock. Tick. Tock.

It was 2 p.m.! I couldn't wait for Izzy.

I hopped on my bike.

"Thanks, Mr. Macintosh! Bye, Zeus!" I called behind me.

If I was lucky, this trail of cupcakes would lead me straight to the scene of the crime!

6 A Crumby Trail

I was still following the trail of crumbs when Izzy caught up with me.

"It's about time," I said.

"It wasn't my fault," Izzy answered. "I thought I was going to be eaten alive while getting a picture of the chicken coop."

"That dog surprised me, too!" I said.

We both laughed.

"The trail stops here," I told Izzy. I pointed down at a glob of yellow icing.

Izzy took a pic. Then she looked around. "Someone trampled those flowers!" she said, pointing.

"Let's check it out!" I said.

We followed the trail of stomped flowers.

It led right to Mrs. Hooper's house! Mrs. Hooper was my piano teacher.

WHERE: Mrs. Hooper's house?

We dropped our bikes and knocked on the door.

No one answered.

I went to the window.

"There's yellow icing on this windowsill!" I exclaimed.

"Mmmm, a clue!" said Izzy, tasting the icing. "Yup, lemon! This matches the cupcake icing in the street!"

"I'm *not* going to ask how you know that," I said, rolling my eyes. "So I bet the thief snuck in through this window . . ."

I stood up on my tippy-toes to see inside.

"What are you doing, Hilde?" Izzy asked.

"Don't worry about me. Just get some shots of that icing smear," I said.

Izzy took pics.

"It's against the law to peep into people's windows," Izzy said. "You're going to get in trouble!"

Right before I could get a look at the crime scene, I saw flashing lights. A police car pulled up.

Click!

 # 7 The Super-Secret Source

A police officer leaned out the car window. Fortunately for me, it was Officer Dee.

He's my only reliable source at the Selinsgrove Police Department. I can always count on him to give me the scoop.

"Hilde, you know you can't peep into people's windows," he called out.

"Sorry, Officer Dee," I answered.

I walked over to his car. Izzy was right behind me.

"Remember, Hilde," he said, "you want to be the one *reporting* the news, not becoming it."

"Yes, Officer Dee," I said. "So are you here about the break-in?"

"No, I'm on my way to another call," he said.

I pulled out my notepad. "Where are you headed?"

"There's some sort of trouble at the Kind Kat Café," he answered. "I've got to go!"

Officer Dee sped away.

WHERE:
* Mrs. Hooper's house
* Kind Kat Café

The Kind Kat Café was my favorite restaurant. Not only is the bacon always crispy, but the owner has three friendly cats.

I hope the cats are okay! I thought.

Izzy and I ran to our bikes.

Just then, Mrs. Hooper pulled into the driveway.

She saw me and smiled. "Hi, Hilde! We aren't scheduled for a lesson today, are we?"

"Hi! No, I'm investigating the break-in," I said. "Can you confirm it happened at your house?"

A reporter always confirms her facts.

Mrs. Hooper's warm smile melted away. "Yes, someone broke into my home early this morning."

"Can you tell me what happened?" I asked.

"I baked cupcakes last night and set them on my kitchen table. When I woke up, that window was open and the plate of cupcakes was gone. Nothing else was stolen. But I still called the police."

I was stumped.

"Why would anyone bother breaking in, only to steal cupcakes?" I asked. "And why didn't they eat them? The thief just threw them in the road."

"I've been asking myself the same questions," replied Mrs. Hooper. "My cupcakes are delicious. That recipe won me the Bake-Off Bonanza three years ago."

I looked at my phone. It was 2:30 p.m.!

"Izzy, we need to get to the Kind Kat Café," I said.

"Thank you, Mrs. Hooper!" we yelled as we hopped on our bikes.

We raced back toward Pine Street.

But then we skidded to a stop!

8 Zeus on the Loose!

Mr. Macintosh and Mrs. Taggert were arguing — right in the middle of the street! Zeus was there, too. He came over and started licking my shoe.

"You and that no-good dog of yours stole my pie!" Mrs. Taggert shouted, wagging her finger. "You knew your cheesecake couldn't beat my cherry crumb pie fair and square, so you cheated! You took it right off my windowsill and fed it to your dog. Fess up!"

Mrs. Taggert might be small, but at that moment she looked like she could win a fight against a brain-eating zombie!

I jotted down everything, waiting to speak.

WHAT: Missing cherry crumb pie
WHERE: Mrs. Taggert's house
WHEN: Within the last hour

"I would never steal your pie!" Mr. Macintosh argued. "And Zeus was on his leash when your pie was stolen. He couldn't have eaten it!"

Mrs. Taggert looked down at Zeus. His little tail hid between his legs.

"Besides," Mr. Macintosh continued. "I don't *need* to cheat to win. I beat you once before and I would've beaten you again this year . . . if someone hadn't stolen my eggs."

"Everyone knows the only reason your cheesecake beat my pie two years ago was because it was a horrible year for cherries," said Mrs. Taggert.

She glared at Mr. Macintosh.

Mr. Macintosh glared back.

Finally, I saw my opportunity to jump in.

"Excuse me, Mr. Macintosh, but earlier today you said, and I quote, 'sweet smells make my animals go crazy! Especially poor Zeus.' Are you —"

"You wrote that down?" he interrupted.

"I'm a reporter. I write everything down," I replied. "So, are you sure Zeus couldn't have had something to do with Mrs. Taggert's missing pie?"

Before Mr. Macintosh could answer, Zeus's leash slipped out of his hand.

"Zeus!" screamed Mr. Macintosh, chasing his dog down the street.

Mrs. Taggert shook her head. "See? He can't control that dog."

"Mrs. Taggert," I said, trying to get my interview back on track. "Where is your pie dish?"

"I have no clue. His wild, pie-stealing dog must've run off with it," she replied.

"What does your dish look like?" I asked.

"It's a blue one-of-a-kind ceramic pie dish with roses painted on it. I'll never be able to replace it," Mrs. Taggert said as she headed home.

"I wish that dog would have saved *me* a piece of pie," Izzy said.

"I don't think Zeus stole the pie," I said. I had a feeling there was more to this sickeningly sweet story . . .

I made a few notes.

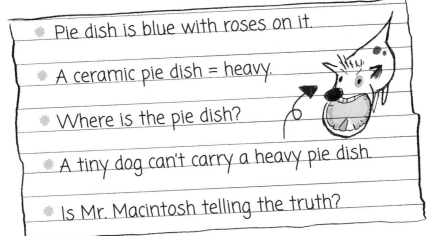

* Pie dish is blue with roses on it.

* A ceramic pie dish = heavy.

* Where is the pie dish?

* A tiny dog can't carry a heavy pie dish.

* Is Mr. Macintosh telling the truth?

"Come on, Hilde. We still have a lead to investigate," said Izzy.

"You're right," I agreed. "Let's get to the Kind Kat Café!"

9 Kind Kat Café

Izzy and I pulled up outside the Kind Kat Café just as Officer Dee drove away. We locked up our bikes.

"Hey, Izzy! Look at this," I said.

A Bake-Off Bonanza poster was taped to the window.

"'All-you-can-eat sweets'? We'd better save room!" Izzy joked.

"Totally," I said. "But check out the prize."

"A thousand dollars?!" Izzy exclaimed. "I should have gone into baking!"

SELINSGROVE
BAKE-OFF BONANZA
AT KIND KAT CAFÉ
$1,000 GRAND PRIZE!

ALL-YOU-CAN-EAT SWEETS!
4 P.M. ~~SATURDAY~~ ToDAY

Glenn, the owner of the café, waved us over. He was holding a garbage bag. His two black cats, Ollie and Mr. Wigglesworth, poked their heads out from behind his legs.

"Hi, Glenn!" I said, leaning down to pet Ollie.

"I was expecting you, Scoop," he said.

Scoop was Glenn's nickname for me. We had become friends because his café was my favorite place to write. He was also a great source.

"I heard you called the police," I said. "What happened?"

"The lunch rush had just ended, so I went into the back to restock things for today's Bake-Off Bonanza. But then I heard something crash to the ground out front. That's when I discovered this," he said.

Glenn dropped the garbage bag on the table.
I heard what sounded like clinking glass.

I peeked inside — and saw the ears from Glenn's special cat-shaped cookie jar!

"I loved that cookie jar!" I cried. "Why would anyone want to break it?"

"I don't know. When I came outside, it was shattered — and cookies were everywhere. Whoever did this left in a rush," Glenn said.

"And after hearing about the crime on Orange Street, I thought it best to call the police."

I wrote everything down.

WHAT: Cookie jar smashed

"Did you see anyone?" Izzy asked.

"Nope," he said, heading inside. "Sorry, girls."

Just then, we spotted Maddy walking toward us.

I know she's a Mean-ager, but a witness is a witness. I took a deep breath.

"Hi, Maddy," I said.

Maddy looked at me like I was gum stuck to the bottom of her shoe.

"Hey, *Hilde*," she said snottily. "How is your cute little baby paper?"

My face turned red. Izzy stepped forward, but I flashed my "I got this" look.

"I'm a serious reporter, Maddy," I said. "Did you happen to see anyone coming or going from the café recently?"

"Well, I saw a small dog run past," Maddy said. "And right before that, I saw Donnie walking down the street."

Izzy and I turned to each other. *Donnie!*

"Remember when Donnie stole from our bake sale?" Izzy whispered to me.

Last summer, Izzy and I held a bake sale. Donnie helped himself to two peanut butter cookies, threw a penny in our money jar, and shouted, "Keep the change!"

NOTES:

* Maddy saw a small dog run past — Could Zeus have knocked over the jar?

* Maddy saw Donnie near the café — Could he be the thief?

I looked at Maddy as she walked away. I wasn't sure I trusted her, considering she's a Mean-ager — just like Donnie and Leon. But a reporter always follows up on a tip.

We headed inside to search for clues.

10 Flat Tire!

Izzy and I took a seat at the counter.

Glenn slid us a plate of bacon. It was super crispy, just the way I like it!

"Thanks, Glenn!" I said, grabbing a piece.

Glenn's spotted cat, Lilly, brushed by my leg. I reached down to give some pets.

Glenn was shuffling papers around, looking for something.

"This isn't good . . ." he said.

"What's wrong, Glenn?" I asked.

"I can't find my list of Bake-Off contestants. I know it was here earlier," he replied. "It's important! That list has every contestant's name, address, and dessert."

"Hmmm," I said, making a note of the missing list.

CLUE: Contestant list — Could it have been stolen?

Tick. Tock. Tick. Tock.

It was 3:20 p.m. My deadline was getting closer!

We headed for the door.

"I hope you find your list, Glenn," Izzy said.

"Thanks, girls," Glenn replied. "And good luck with your story, Scoop!"

As soon as we stepped outside, Izzy froze.

"Hilde, your bike!" she exclaimed.

Both of my bike tires were flat. Someone had put holes in them!

At first I felt angry. But then I smiled.

"Why are you smiling?" Izzy asked.

"Because this means the thief knows I'm hot on his — or her — heels," I said. "Besides, Dad can patch these tires up, no problem."

"I guess you're right, but this person could be dangerous," Izzy said. "Do you think it was Donnie?"

"Maybe," I said. "Let's review our notes so far."

I sat down. Izzy pulled up a chair.

I opened my notepad . . .

WHEN?

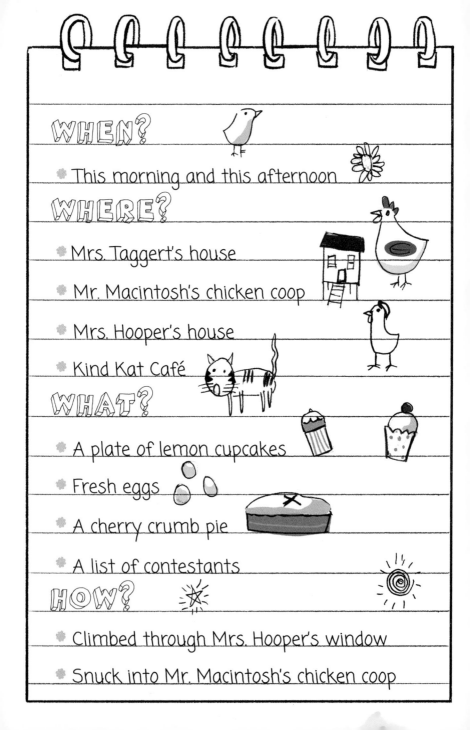

* This morning and this afternoon

WHERE?

* Mrs. Taggert's house

* Mr. Macintosh's chicken coop

* Mrs. Hooper's house

* Kind Kat Café

WHAT?

* A plate of lemon cupcakes

* Fresh eggs

* A cherry crumb pie

* A list of contestants

HOW?

* Climbed through Mrs. Hooper's window

* Snuck into Mr. Macintosh's chicken coop

* Swiped pie from Mrs. Taggert's windowsill

* Snuck into café while Glenn was in the back

WHO?

Donnie:

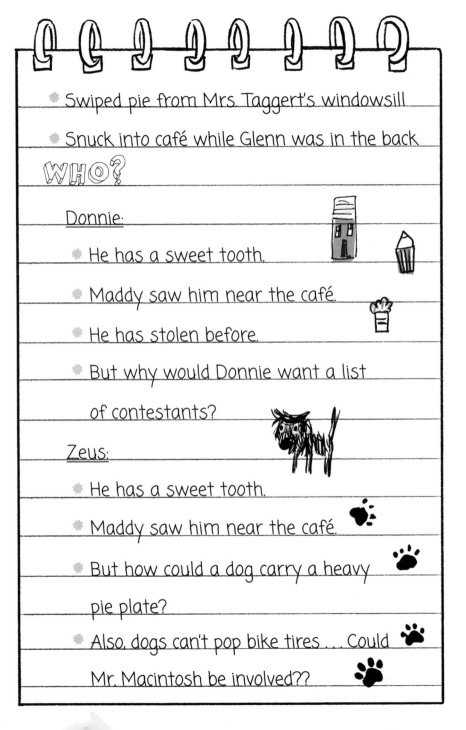

* He has a sweet tooth.

* Maddy saw him near the café.

* He has stolen before.

* But why would Donnie want a list

of contestants?

Zeus:

* He has a sweet tooth.

* Maddy saw him near the café.

* But how could a dog carry a heavy

pie plate?

* Also, dogs can't pop bike tires... Could

Mr. Macintosh be involved??

Izzy looked puzzled.

"I don't think Mr. Macintosh is the thief," she said. "His eggs were stolen, remember?"

"I remember," I said, looking up from my notes. "But I'm not certain Donnie's the thief. And some clues do point to Zeus or Mr. Macintosh . . ."

"What are you going to do? Interview the dog?" Izzy said, laughing.

My older sister thinks she's just *sooo* funny.

"Get serious, Izzy," I said. "We need to find a way to *prove* who the thief is."

"Okay, but we don't have a lot of time," she replied.

We both looked at our phones. It was 3:50 p.m.

"You're right. Our deadline is only two hours away, and the Bake-Off Bonanza is about to start," I said. "But since we *know* the thief has a sweet tooth, and since the stolen items all seem to be related to the contest, today's Bake-Off could be the perfect place to catch our thief!"

"Good thinking!" Izzy answered, jumping up.

"Come on! There isn't a second to lose!" I said.

11 The Chase

Izzy and I ran around to the front of the café. Bakers were setting up their desserts.

"So who do you think is going to win the thousand-dollar prize?" asked Izzy.

"I don't know," I said. "Without Mrs. Taggert's cherry crumb pie or Mr. Macintosh's cheesecake, this year's contest is wide open!"

"I would have voted for Mrs. Hooper's lemon cupcakes, but those are gone, too," Izzy said. She took out her camera. "Now, where should we look for our thief?"

"Let's check the tables first to see if we notice anything out of the ordinary," I said.

We were walking along the second row of tables when I stopped in my tracks.

"No way," I said. I grabbed Izzy and we ducked behind a table. "Look over there!"

Maddy was there. She was setting up a table with a red-and-white checkered tablecloth. In the center was a pie.

"I didn't know Maddy knew how to bake," said Izzy, taking a pic.

"Me either," I said.

"Yum!" said Izzy. "It looks like her pie has a crumb topping on it."

"Wait a minute," I whispered. "What if Maddy's our thief? Could that pie be Mrs. Taggert's cherry crumb pie?"

"I don't think so," Izzy replied. "Maddy's pie dish is red. See?"

"You're right," I agreed, checking my notes. "Mrs. Taggert said her pie dish was blue with roses painted on it."

We continued scanning tables.

People started taking their seats, so we headed toward the stage.

Mr. Macintosh, Mrs. Taggert, and Mrs. Hooper were all seated up front. I saw Donnie and Leon toward the back.

At 4 p.m. sharp, Mayor Jeff stepped up to the microphone. "Welcome to Selinsgrove's Bake-Off Bonanza, the most delicious day of the year! Bakers, get ready! The judges are about to come around!"

I looked over at Maddy. She seemed to be inspecting her pie. She suddenly picked it up and dashed behind the Kind Kat Café.

Just then, I saw something black dart after her. It was dragging a leash.

"Did you see that?!" I asked.

"Yeah, so?" said Izzy. "Maddy's probably just going to use the restroom."

"No, behind her!" I cried. "I think Zeus is chasing Maddy!"

"Oh, no!" Izzy cried. "He's going to steal *her* pie, too?!"

"We're about to crack this case wide open!" I said as we ran after them.

12 GRRRRRRRUFFFF!

We got around back just in time to see Maddy opening the back door — with Zeus closing in fast!

"Maddy, watch out behind you!" yelled Izzy.

It was too late. The door had already closed, and Zeus had slipped in behind her.

I yanked open the door and burst inside.

Izzy was right behind me.

At first, all I could see was Mr. Wigglesworth and Ollie in their favorite hiding place underneath the front table.

Then I spotted Maddy behind the counter, holding her pie up high. Zeus kept jumping up to try to get it!

"Get this dog away from me!" screamed Maddy. Her eyes were the size of pancakes.

GRRRRRUFFF!

Zeus's bark was so loud that Maddy jumped.

She lost her balance and her pie tumbled to the ground.

Cherries and sugar crumb topping flew in every direction. The pie dish shattered.

I thought Zeus would head right for the spilled dessert. But he kept barking at Maddy.

GRRRRRRRRRRRRRUFFF!
GRRRRRRRRRRRRRUFFF!

"Get off me!" said Maddy, pushing the small dog away. She tried to climb onto the counter to escape.

But she slipped on some cherries and fell to the floor.

Zeus leapt on top of her!

"Zeus! No!" I yelled.

Izzy took some pics.

Zeus wagged his tail as he began licking something on Maddy's shirt.

The front door flew open. Glenn and Mr. Macintosh rushed in.

"We heard screaming. Is everyone okay?" Glenn asked. He looked down at the mess. "What happened in here?"

Maddy pointed her finger at Zeus. "I'll tell you what happened! That dog chased me and knocked my pie right out of my hand!"

"Zeus!" yelled Mr. Macintosh. "I can't believe your behavior today. Mrs. Taggert was right about you. You've been a very bad dog!"

He scooped Zeus up off the ground.

"Your mutt ruined my pie that I spent *hours* baking!" Maddy told Mr. Macintosh. "Now I can't win the contest!"

Zeus growled at Maddy.

More people rushed inside to see what all the yelling was about. Mrs. Hooper shook her head when she saw the mess. Mayor Jeff was there, too, nervously rubbing his fingers together. Standing nearby were Donnie and Leon.

Officer Wentworth had arrived, too. He looked as grumpy as ever.

"Zeus is my responsibility," said Mr. Macintosh. "I should've had a tighter grip on his leash. I'm sorry, Maddy."

Maddy narrowed her eyes. "Well, I certainly hope you're sorry," she said. "You and your dog ruined everything!"

"I'll get this mess cleaned up," said Glenn. He started brushing cherries, crumbs, and the broken pie dish into a dustpan, when I spotted something — a flash of blue and a tiny pink rose.

"Stop!" I yelled.

13 Breaking News!

I picked up a broken piece of the pie dish.

"Zeus isn't a pie-stealing dog!" I said. "He's a hero!"

Maddy turned to me, hands on hips.

"Some reporter you are, Hilde!" she said. "You can't even see a bad *dog* when he's right in front of your face!"

"Now hold on," said Glenn, stepping forward. "If Zeus wasn't after Maddy's pie, Scoop, then why did he chase her?"

"Because Maddy stole that pie!" I shouted, pulling out my notepad. "She's a thief!"

Everyone turned to look at Maddy.

"You have no proof," said Maddy, smiling. "A cute little baby reporter like you should leave crime solving to the grown-ups."

I felt so angry. I didn't know what to say.

She took a step closer. "You should really stick to what you know — like tea parties!"

Just then, Izzy snapped another picture of Maddy — this time two inches from her face.

"Hey!" Maddy screamed.

Officer Wentworth stepped in between Maddy and Izzy. Then he turned toward me. "If you are going to make a serious accusation like that, Hilde, you need proof."

"I have all the proof I need," I said, holding up the broken piece of the pie dish.

I peeled back the sticky red paint, revealing the blue color underneath.

"That wasn't Maddy's cherry crumb pie!" I said. "It was Mrs. Taggert's!"

Mrs. Taggert pushed her way forward.

"Well — I'll be," she stammered, examining the broken piece. "That *is* my dish!"

"The proof is in the pie . . . or the pie dish!" Mr. Macintosh exclaimed.

Maddy looked like she was trying to think of something to say, but nothing came out.

"Maddy knew she didn't have a chance of winning the Bake-Off Bonanza with *her* baking," I continued. "So she stole Mrs. Taggert's pie, painted the dish red, and entered it as her own! I bet she just came in here to touch up her paint job."

"This is ridiculous!" shouted Maddy. "I didn't paint that dish. I *bought* it. Aren't 'reporters' supposed to check their facts?"

My face reddened.

Just then, Izzy spoke up. "We have proof that Maddy stole more than just Mrs. Taggert's pie."

Izzy pulled up a picture for everyone to see. "Look," she said, zooming in. "There was yellow icing on Mrs. Hooper's windowsill."

"And look," I added. "What do you all see on Maddy's shirt?"

Mrs. Hooper gasped. She rushed forward to take a closer look. There was a yellow smudge on Maddy's shirt.

"That's my icing!" she said. "She stole my cupcakes!"

Then Mr. Macintosh stepped forward.

"That means you stole my eggs, too, didn't you?" he demanded. "So that I couldn't make my cheesecake?"

Maddy's fists were clenched. Her face was as red as the spilled cherries by her feet.

"Okay, okay!" cried Officer Wentworth. "Everyone calm down. Why would Maddy do all these things?"

I looked down at my notepad. Suddenly, all the puzzle pieces fit together.

"I know why," I said.

14 *Cute* Enough for You?

"**M**addy needed money to buy concert tickets," I explained. "She thought she could trip up the other contestants, enter Mrs. Taggert's pie as her own, and pocket the one-thousand-dollar prize. She even swiped Glenn's list of contestants just to make sure she wouldn't have any surprise competition."

"And when we spotted Maddy near the café earlier today, she knew we were close to figuring out the truth," Izzy added. "That's why she pointed the finger at Zeus and Donnie."

"It's also why she slashed my bike tires!" I added.

The crowd gasped. Donnie and Leon's jaws dropped.

Finally, Maddy exploded. "Yes, I did it! I wanted to use the prize money to buy tickets to see Noise Pollution. And if it weren't for this *cute* little baby reporter, I would've gotten away with it!" she said. "I just wanted to go to the concert with my friends. Noise Pollution never comes to Selinsgrove, and the tickets are so expensive!"

"That's called a confession!" I said, taking a step closer to Maddy. "There, is that *cute* enough for you?"

I coolly raised my hand in the air and Izzy slapped it five. Then I wrote down what Maddy had said, word for word.

Mr. Macintosh shook his head. "This was all for a rock concert?"

Maddy looked down. She knew she had been caught.

Officer Wentworth stepped forward. "You damaged people's property and stole from them. This is very serious, Maddy. You'll have to come with me. We'll call your parents from the police station."

Izzy took more pics as Officer Wentworth walked Maddy outside.

"Mystery solved, Hilde!" Izzy said.

Then Mrs. Taggert walked up to Mr. Macintosh. She pulled a bundle of oatmeal raisin cookies from her picnic basket.

"I'm sorry for jumping to conclusions," she said. "I hope these make up for my rude behavior."

"They sure do," Mr. Macintosh said.

Glenn smiled at Izzy and me. "You two figured this all out by yourselves?"

"We sure did!" Izzy answered.

"You girls are not just great reporters," he said. "You're heroes!"

I looked over at Zeus, who was back in Mr. Macintosh's arms.

"Zeus is the real hero," I said. "If that brave little dog hadn't come along when he did, Maddy would've won the contest and gotten away with everything."

I looked at the clock. 5:20 p.m.!

"Izzy! Hand me your computer right now!"

I typed up my story super fast, but not too fast. A reporter always double-checks quotes and makes sure everything is spelled correctly.

Izzy scrolled through the pictures on her camera and inserted the best ones.

"Nice work, Izzy," I said.

"This story is front-page news!" Izzy said, reading it over.

But my news article wasn't finished yet. I knew readers would want to know who won the Bake-Off Bonanza . . .

Just then, Mrs. Hooper popped inside. "Come on, girls!" she said. "Mayor Jeff is about to announce the winners!"

15 Hero Dog

Izzy and I ran outside just as Mayor Jeff was opening a golden envelope.

"Ladies and gentlemen," he announced. "This year's Bake-Off Bonanza winner is Mr. Macintosh — for his eggless brownies!"

Everyone clapped as Mr. Macintosh climbed onto the stage and accepted his prize. Zeus stood by his side. Izzy took a picture.

"Now," continued Mayor Jeff, "there is one last order of business before you dive into dessert. I'd like everyone to meet Selinsgrove's star reporters: Hilde and Izzy Lysiak!"

"Is he talking about us?!" Izzy asked.

I couldn't believe it either!

Mayor Jeff waved us up on stage.

"By now, I'm sure everyone has heard what happened at the Kind Kat Café today. Hilde's reporting skills and Izzy's pictures really saved our contest," he said. "We're so glad you cracked the case!"

Everyone cheered as he handed Izzy and me our very own press passes.

The passes had our names and pictures on them! Then Mayor Jeff put a medal on Zeus.

I leaned down to hug him, and he wagged his tail.

As Izzy and I walked off the stage, we spotted Officer Dee.

We ran over to him.

"What will happen to Maddy?" I asked.

"Don't worry about her," he answered. "No one is pressing charges. But she will have to figure out a way to repay everyone."

I picked up my pen.

Officer Dee raised an eyebrow. "Don't quote me on that, Hilde."

It was time to put the finishing touches on my article. I pulled the laptop out of Izzy's bag and posted our story at 5:58 p.m. Two whole minutes ahead of deadline!

Just then, an important call came on Officer Dee's radio.

"A *what?!*" he cried. "I'm on my way!"

"What's up, Officer Dee?" I asked.

"I've got to go!" he said. "There is a bear on the loose in Selinsgrove!"

Izzy and I looked at each other.

"Let's go!" I shouted.

I grabbed two snickerdoodles from a table nearby. (A reporter can't work on an empty stomach!)

Then we jumped on Izzy's bike.

"Do you think there's *really* a bear loose?" Izzy asked.

"In the news business," I said, "anything is possible!"

HERO DOG NABS BAKED GOODS THIEF![1]

BY HILDE KATE LYSIAK

A teenage girl was busted for trying to cheat her way to victory in the Selinsgrove Bake-Off Bonanza, by a heroic dog![2]

Maddy Marie, 16, confessed to stealing several baked goods. But Zeus, a small dog, chased down a stolen pie belonging to Mrs. Taggert.[3]

PHOTO CREDIT: ISABEL ROSE LYSIAK

"Yes, I did it!" Maddy confessed to the *Orange Street News*. "I wanted to use the prize money to buy tickets to see Noise Pollution." 4

PHOTO CREDIT: ISABEL ROSE LYSIAK

After the shocking confession, Mayor Jeff announced that Mr. Macintosh's eggless brownies won this year's Bake-Off Bonanza. 5

No formal charges are expected to be filed against Maddy, a source told the *Orange Street News*. 6

1. HEADLINE 2. LEDE 3. NUT 4. QUOTE 5. SUPPORT 6. KICKER

WHO? Hilde Lysiak

WHAT? Hilde is the real-life publisher of her own newspaper, the *Orange Street News*! You can read her work at www.orangestreetnews.com.

WHEN? Hilde began her newspaper when she was seven years old with crayons and paper. Today, she has millions of readers!

WHERE? Hilde lives in Selinsgrove, Pennsylvania.

WHY? Hilde loves adventure, is super curious, and believes that you don't have to be a grown-up to do great things in the world!

HOW? Tips from people just like you make Hilde's newspaper possible!

Matthew Lysiak is Hilde's dad and coauthor. He is a former reporter for the *New York Daily News*.

Joanne Lew-Vriethoff was born in Malaysia and grew up in Los Angeles. She received her B.A. in illustration from Art Center College of Design in Pasadena. Today, Joanne lives in Amsterdam, where she spends much of her time illustrating children's books.

Hilde Cracks the Case

HERO DOG!

Questions & Activities

1) What are the **six** questions Hilde has to answer in order to write a news story and solve a case?

2) Reread the Introduction. Why does Hilde create a newspaper for her town?

3) Turn to the Reporter's Toolbox on page 2 and find the word *source*. Name a *source* from the story. What information did he or she give to Hilde?

4) What does Zeus do that makes him a hero?

5) Think about something interesting that happened at school, at home, or in your neighborhood. Answer all six questions (see question #1 above). Then write your own news story!

READY TO CRACK THE NEXT CASE?

Here is a **SNEAK PEEK** of the second book in the series! This is a *super-special* sneak peek where you get to see the illustrator's early sketches for the book. To learn more about the illustrator and about how sketches turn into final artwork, please go to page 102.

1 Police Chase!

Officer Dee looked like a blur of blue as he sprinted down Market Street.

My older sister, Izzy, pedaled while I stood on her bike pegs. We raced to catch up to the police officer. Officer Dee is my most reliable source at the Selinsgrove Police Department.

"Do you really think there's a bear in town?" Izzy asked.

It may sound crazy, but Izzy and I had both heard the same thing: Officer Dee had said he got a call there was a bear on the loose in Selinsgrove.

"Every tip needs to be confirmed!" I called up to her. "That means finding the facts. Pedal faster, Izzy!"

My heart was racing. People love animal stories — and a good story with a picture of a bear in it could be our biggest story yet!

Izzy pumped her legs harder. "I'm pedaling as fast as I can!" she said.

Officer Dee took a right on Pine. I clung to Izzy's shoulders as she made a sharp turn.

I had a good tip about *what* happened: *A bear was on the loose.* But I needed a lot more answers if I wanted to have a story fit for *the Orange Street News.*

Who? What? When? Where? Why? How?

Officer Dee was fast.
But Izzy on a bike was faster.

We were catching up when he ran onto the grass beside Grove Grocer.

Grove Grocer is the most popular store in town. Their famous beef jerky is one of my all-time favorite snacks.

"Officer Dee just ran behind the store!" Izzy said.

I hopped off Izzy's bike.

"Come on! Let's investigate," I said.

We ran behind Grove Grocer — and couldn't believe what we saw next!

2 The First Clue

Banana peels, coffee grounds, cardboard boxes, and all kinds of trash dotted the green grass behind Grove Grocer. It looked like a tornado had struck a garbage truck full of, well, garbage! The mess stretched all the way back to Selinsgrove Forest!

"Gross!" Izzy said. She began taking pictures.

I spotted Officer Dee right away. He was already busy talking to Mr. Troutman, the owner of Grove Grocer. The two of them were pointing to a red bird feeder lying on the ground.

Why are they staring at a bird feeder?

A reporter
knows to never interrupt
a police officer during an interview.
But I still had to investigate. I pulled out my
notepad and stood off to the side, listening.

I tried to get a good look at the feeder. And
when I did, my eyes almost bulged out of my head!

The black metal pole that held up the feeder
looked like it had been pulled out of the ground.
Instead of a straight line, it was twisted into the
shape of an L.

I got Izzy's attention and pointed at the feeder. She ran over and said, "It looks like that thing was tossed by an angry dinosaur!"

We bent down for a closer look . . .

There were five large scratch marks on the feeder!

I jotted some notes.

Finally, Officer Dee walked away from Mr. Troutman. He nodded at me before he began inspecting the scene. That was his way of letting me know he was finished with the witness.

I saw my opening.

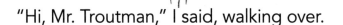

"Hi, Mr. Troutman," I said, walking over.

"Hi, Hilde," he said. "If you are looking for beef jerky, you'll have to come back tomorrow. I closed up early — so I can clean up this mess."

"I'm actually here on business," I said, pointing to my press pass. "I'm reporting for my newspaper, the *Orange Street News.* I wanted to ask you some questions about what happened today."

"Sure. Well, I was inside getting ready to close the store, when I heard loud clanging noises," he said.

"Clanging noises?" I asked.

"Yeah, it sounded like someone was banging on my garbage cans like they were drums," he added.

"What happened next?" I asked.

"I walked around back, expecting to yell at some rowdy teenagers," Mr. Troutman continued. "But that's when I saw it!"

3 Mangled and Clawed!

"What did you see, Mr. Troutman?" I asked.

I held my pen to my notepad.

"That's when I saw my mangled bird feeder," said Mr. Troutman. "And when I took a closer look, I found *this* stuck to the feeder!"

He held up a small tuft of black fur.

"What is it?" I asked.

"I'm no animal expert, but I believe it's fur from a large bear!" he said.

To be continued . . .

Artwork: Behind the Scenes!

Learn more about Joanne Lew-Vriethoff, the illustrator behind Hilde Cracks the Case!

Joanne's studio

What made you want to be an illustrator?

Ever since I was a kid, I've had an active imagination. It drove my teachers crazy when I wasn't paying attention in class, but my daydreams gave me lots of ideas for fun things to draw. I love making art that tells stories people can connect with emotionally.

How do you create an illustration?

First, I think about what I want my art to say. Then I start sketching. I draw a more-final piece in pen and ink. Next, I scan it into my computer. Finally, I add the colors digitally. My favorite part of the process is the beginning — when my ideas form.

sketch

final art

Where do your ideas come from?

My daydreams — and my real-life travels, too! I love traveling with my kids and my husband. We have visited ancient monasteries in Spain, explored castles in France, biked along the canals in Amsterdam, and even snorkeled in Asia. One of my all-time favorite things to do is wander tiny streets at night when everything feels magical.

Joanne with her son and daughter

BRANCHES™

WHICH BOOKS HAVE YOU READ?

HILDE CRACKS THE CASE
by Hilde Lysiak, with Matthew Lysiak
illustrated by Joanne Lew-Vriethoff

DRAGON MASTERS
by Tracey West

THE NOTEBOOK OF DOOM
by Troy Cummings

HELP ME BATTLE MONSTERS!

■SCHOLASTIC
scholastic.com/branches

Available in print
and eBook editions

EERIE ELEMENTARY
by Jack Chabert

MY SCHOOL IS SO CREEPY!

THE LAST FIREHAWK
by Katrina Charman
illustrated by Jeremy Norton

THE AMAZING STARDUST FRIENDS by Heather Alexander

STELLA AND THE NIGHT SPRITES by Sam Hay

LOONIVERSE
by David Lubar

SILVER PONY RANCH
by D.L. Green

LOTUS LANE
by Kyla May

MEET MY COOL FRIENDS!

SCHOLASTIC
scholastic.com/branches

Available in print
and eBook editions